This one's for Harry

P.H.

For P & p
Love D

First published in Great Britain 2005
This book and audio edition published 2007
by Egmont UK Limited
239 Kensington High Street,
London W8 6SA

Text copyright © Peter Harris 2005
Illustrations copyright © Deborah Allwright 2005
Music and lyrics copyright © Barry Gibson 2007
Recording copyright © Egmont UK Limited 2007

The moral rights of the author, illustrator
and composer have been asserted

A CIP catalogue for this title is available
from The British Library

ISBN 978 1 4052 3043 8

1 3 5 7 9 10 8 6 4 2

Printed in Singapore

JP

THE NIGHT PIRATES

Peter Harris

Deborah Allwright

EGMONT

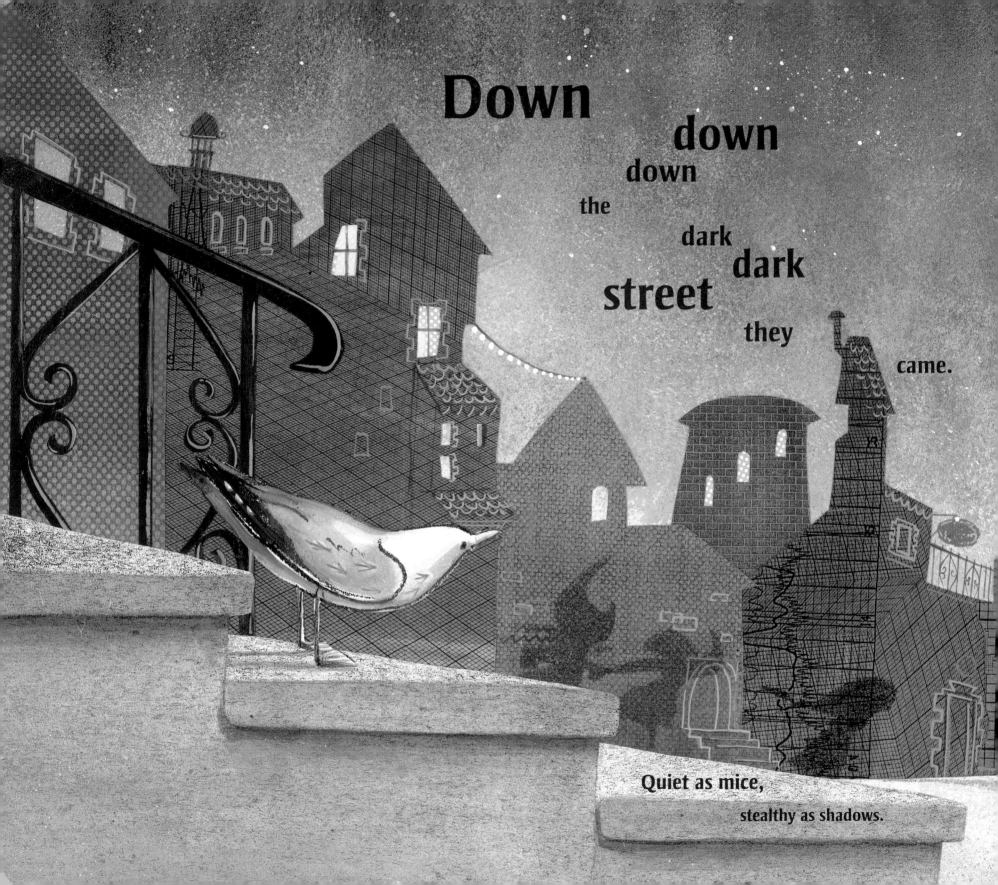

Down
down
down
the
dark
dark
street
they
came.

Quiet as mice,
stealthy as shadows.

Up

up

up

the

dark

dark

house

they
climbed.

Stealthy as
shadows,
quiet as mice.

Only the moon
was watching them
when they arrived.

Only the moon
was watching them
when they left.

Only the moon . . .

. . . and one little boy.

Tom was a nice little boy.
Tom was a brave little boy.
Tom was a little boy about to have **an adventure.**

Who were these shadows
as quiet as mice
**stealing away with
the front of Tom's house?**

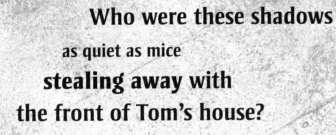

**Maybe monsters
or trolls?**

**Maybe ogres
or gremlins?**

PIRATES!

Rough, tough little *girl pirates*.
With their own pirate ship.

A ship set for sailing.
A ship off on adventures.
A ship stealing the front
of Tom's house
for disguise!

But what about Tom?
Could he join the crew?

"Please

let me aboard!

Can I come too?"

And did the *girl captain* **say,**
"*Certainly not!*
You're only a boy!"

Oh no, not at all!
Instead she **roared,**

"Welcome aboard!"

Then **up** went the sails
and **up** went the flag.

Then off sailed the **rough**,
tough little *girl pirates*.

The little *girl pirates*
and their shipmate
Tom.

But where were they going?

To an island.

Where *Captain Patch*
and his **really rough,**
tough GROWN-UP pirates
were snoozing around their
full treasure chest.

Then *Captain Patch* saw **something.**

Something
very
strange.

Something very strange **indeed.**

What could he see?

A house
sailing
towards them,

getting closer
and **closer**.

A house sailing
towards them,
with a little boy
waving hello!

"I've seen a house!" *Captain Patch* declared.
"We've all seen houses," said the pirates. "Who cares?"

"Don't just lie there. Do something!" *Captain Patch* roared.
But the pirates went back to sleep and just snored,
while the house sailed nearer and nearer until . . .

. . . out **leapt** the *girl pirates!*

And out leapt Tom!

And out leapt a fearsome roar!

The pirates gaped.

The pirates goggled.

Then the
pirates
all
r
a n
a
w
a
y
!

So Tom
and the *girl pirates*
sailed away with
the treasure . . .

. . . while the
**rough, tough
GROWN-UP**
pirates
hid in
the
trees.

Captain Patch stamped his feet and shouted his **worst** pirate curse.

"If you don't give me my treasure back, I'll tell my MUM!"

But off they had sailed,
all the way home.

Down
down
down
the
dark
dark
street
they
came.

Quiet as mice,
stealthy as shadows.

Up

up

up

the

dark

dark

house

they
climbed.

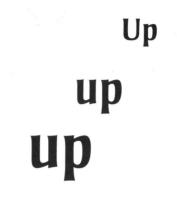

Stealthy as shadows,

quiet as mice.

Only the moon
was watching them
when they arrived.

Only the moon
was watching them
when they left.

Only the
moon . . .

. . . and one little boy.

Tom was a brave little boy.

Tom was a sleepy little boy.

Tom was a boy who had had an adventure.

And no one would ever find out . . .

. . . would they?

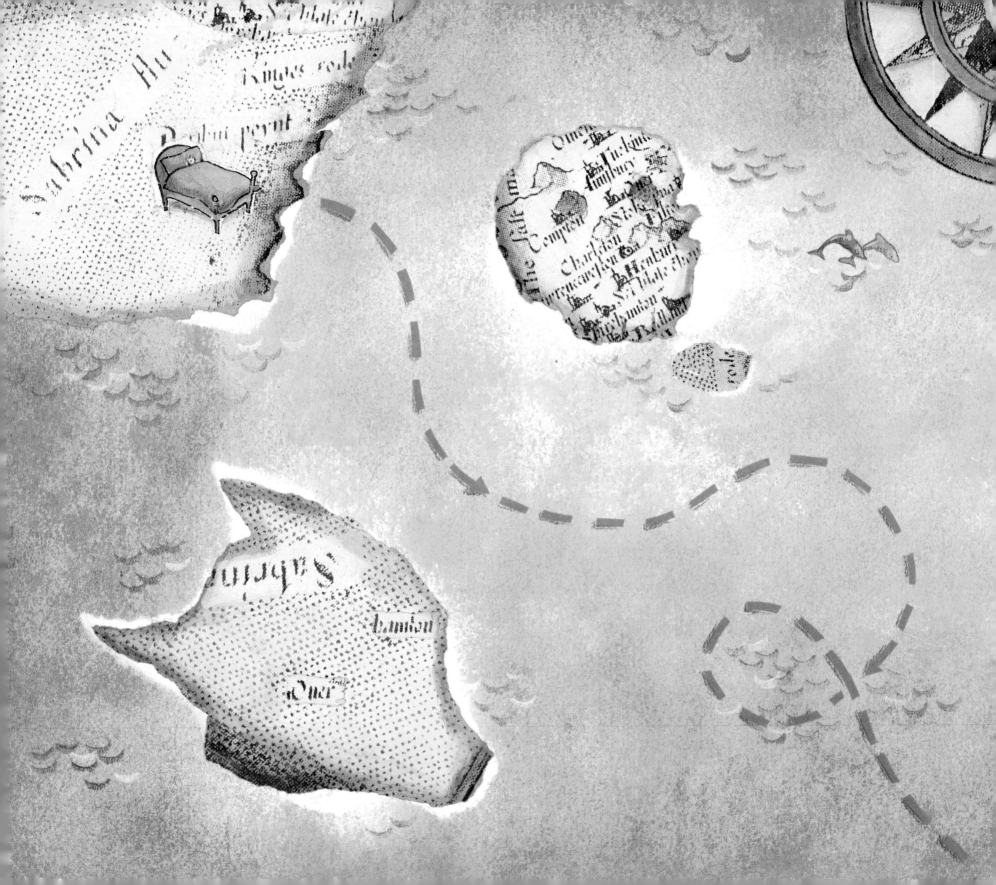